W9-BWO-450

StarFriends
POISON POTION

To Mia Daunt—who writes great stories
and loves Star Friends!—L.C.

To Lola—L.F.

tiger tales

5 River Road, Suite 128, Wilton, CT 06897
Published in the United States 2021
Originally published in Great Britain 2019
by the Little Tiger Group

ISBN-13: 978-1-6643-4000-8
ISBN-10: 1-6643-4000-9
Printed in the USA
STP/4800/0413/0621

2 4 6 8 10 9 7 5 3 1

www.tigertalesbooks.com

POISON POTION

BY LINDA CHAPMAN
ILLUSTRATED BY LUCY FLEMING

tiger tales

Contents

1
In The Star World

Deep in the glittering woods, an owl, a stag, a badger, and a wolf stood around a pool of stars watching a picture in the sparkling surface. It showed four ten-year-old girls, each cuddling an animal—a fox, a squirrel, a wildcat, and a deer. The animals all had beautiful indigo eyes.

"Mia, Lexi, Violet, and Sita," said the wolf. "They're turning out to be excellent Star Friends."

"Indeed. They are doing a lot of good in the human world by using magic," agreed the owl. "Their Star Animals are helping them discover new abilities and develop their powers."

Every so often, young animals from the Star World would travel to the human world. When they got there, they had to find a child who believed in magic enough to be their Star Friend. Each animal taught their Star Friend how to connect with the magical current that ran between the human world and the Star World, and then the child had to use it to help others and stop people who wanted to use magic to do evil things.

"Our young Star Animals look very happy with their friends," said the badger.

"They are, but they are also facing a dangerous threat at the moment," said the owl. "The person doing dark magic near them is very powerful, although they do not know who she is yet."

"A battle is coming," said the wolf.

The owl nodded gravely. "And it is fast approaching."

The stag looked anxious. "Let us hope our animals and their friends can win."

2
A Strange Dream

I must be dreaming. Mia shivered as she looked around. She was standing in the woods dressed only in her pajamas. The sky had just the faintest hint of dawn light in the east.

I want to wake up, Mia thought firmly. *Wake up now!* But she didn't. Through the trees, she could see the clearing where she had first met Bracken, her fox who had come from the Star World. She started walking toward it but then stopped. A cloaked figure was standing in the center of the clearing, surrounded by a green circle of light. She was tearing up leaves and dropping them into a silver bowl. A chill crept up Mia's spine. She had a feeling something bad was going to happen. *Wake up,* she told herself quickly. *Just wake up!*

But she remained in the woods.

"Creeping ivy … ground elder … nightshade…," muttered the woman as she dropped the plant leaves. A large hood concealed her face. *"Come together, merge together, give me power to bind forever…."*

She waved her hand over the bowl, and green smoke spiraled up. Then she pointed at a bush nearby. Small pink and white flowers suddenly bloomed all over it, buds bursting open as if it were a summer's day instead of a cold winter's night.

Picking the flowers, the woman added them to the bowl. *"And to seal the spell,"* she said. The smoke thickened, and a bitter smell wafted toward Mia's nostrils.

"Give me your power, trees!" the woman cried.

A cold wind swept around the clearing, blowing Mia's shoulder-length, dark-blond hair around her face and pulling at her pajama legs. She could feel magic crackling through the air, prickling her skin like needles. The trees shook, and then there was a bright flash of light inside the bowl, and the clearing became still again.

The woman laughed, and taking a silver bottle from her pocket, she filled it with dark liquid from the bowl. Then she straightened and held it up to the stars. "For those who would meddle in my affairs," she said grimly. "They will be sorry."

Mia felt intense foreboding sweep over her as she looked at the little silver bottle in the woman's hands.

With a laugh, the woman tucked it into a pocket of her cloak and strode from the clearing. She passed Mia without seeming to notice her, her dark cloak swishing around her ankles....

Mia woke, her heart pounding. A damp nose was snuffling at her cheek. "Are you okay?" She found herself gazing into Bracken's indigo-blue eyes. "Were you having a nightmare?" he asked anxiously.

She nodded and sat up, looking around the room. She was having a sleepover with her friends at Violet's house. Violet's Star Animal, Sorrel, the wildcat, was stretched out at her feet. Lexi was sleeping in a sleeping bag with Juniper, the squirrel, snuggled against her chest, while Sita, like Mia, was sleeping on an inflatable bed on the floor. Willow, the deer, was lying beside Sita, her delicate legs curled underneath her, her head resting on Sita's back. They looked very peaceful. Mia pulled Bracken into her arms and rubbed his soft, russet-red fur. His black whiskers tickled her skin.

"Was it a magic nightmare?" he asked as he cuddled closer.

Mia pushed back her hair as she remembered it. "It was."

The Star Animals had shown Mia and her friends how to use the current of Star Magic in order to do magic themselves. The girls all had different magical abilities. Violet could create illusions, shadow-travel, and command Shades to return to the shadows where they belonged; Lexi could use magic to be incredibly agile and run super-fast; Sita could heal and soothe, and also had the ability to command people to do whatever she wanted, although she found that power frightening and almost never used it; and Mia's abilities had to do with sight. She could use a shiny surface to see what was happening in other places and to see into the past and future, and her dreams often showed her things that were useful.

"What did you see?" Bracken asked.

Mia told him.

"You've had a dream like this before, haven't you?" Bracken said.

"Kind of, but not exactly the same," said Mia. The last time she had seen the cloaked figure in a dream, the figure had also been drawing energy from the surrounding trees and using it to make a potion. "There was less wind this time and no lightning, and the person made a bush bloom with flowers and then used the flowers in a potion she was making. She said words that sounded like a spell." She shivered as she remembered the silver bottle the person had held up. "I don't know what she was doing, but it felt like very bad magic."

"We'd better tell the others," said Bracken anxiously.

Mia glanced up at the window. Pale light was starting to streak across the night sky. "Okay, let's wake them up." She went around the room, gently shaking her friends' shoulders while Bracken woke the Star Animals. He nuzzled Juniper and Willow awake, but when it came to Sorrel, he gave her long tabby tail a playful tug.

She sprang up with a hiss and glared at him. "What are you doing, Fox?" she spat. "How dare you pull my—"

"Mia had a dream," Bracken interrupted. "I had to wake you up quickly. Come on, pussycat."

Leaving Sorrel with her fur puffed up, he leaped back into Mia's arms. She shook her head at him but couldn't help smiling. He and Sorrel had a prickly relationship. The wildcat could be very arrogant, and Bracken could be a tease.

Soon, the girls were all sitting on Mia's inflatable bed, their comforters over their legs, cuddling their animals and listening as she recounted her dream.

"So, you were in the woods, and you saw someone making a potion?" said Violet.

"Was it definitely the same person you've seen before?" asked Sita, petting Willow's velvety, dappled-brown coat.

"Definitely," said Mia. "I couldn't see her face, but I'm sure it was the same person."

"The one who's been doing dark magic in the clearing, making potions and conjuring Shades," said Willow with a shiver.

Mia nodded. The clearing was a crossing point between the human world and the Star World, so the magic current was very strong there. A few weeks ago, the girls and animals had discovered that the clearing was withering—the spring flowers and green buds were shriveling up. The animals suspected it was because someone was doing dark magic in the clearing, draining its power. Mia's dreams and visions had seemed to back this up.

"Do you think you were seeing something that has happened in the past, or was it something that will happen in the future, Mia?" Lexi said. "Your dreams can show either, can't they?"

Mia nodded. "I don't know which one it was."

"You said it was almost morning in your dream," said Violet thoughtfully, glancing at her bedroom window. "Well, the sun is just rising now. Could you have been seeing the present?"

Mia hadn't thought about that possibility.

"I guess.... I *was* wearing these pajamas," she said slowly.

"So you could have been seeing what was actually happening as it was happening?" said Bracken, pricking his ears. "That's a clever idea, Violet!"

"Of course it is," said Sorrel. She purred and pressed herself against Violet's chest. "Violet *always* has excellent ideas."

Violet looked happy. "If it just happened, there might still be some clues in the clearing—clues that will help us figure out who this person is," she said eagerly. "We might find a footprint, or the person might have dropped something." She pushed her comforter back. "We could go and look."

"Okay!" said Mia, jumping to her feet.

"But what if your mom comes in here, Violet?" said Lexi.

"I'll leave a note saying we wanted to go for an early morning walk, and I'll take my phone so she can call me if she's worried," said Violet. "It'll be fine."

"Um ... what if we go there and the person comes back?" said Sita.

"Even better. Then we'll know who she is, and you'll be able to use your magic to command her to stop!" said Violet.

"Oh ... okay," said Sita, looking a little alarmed.

"Come on, everyone, get dressed!" Violet insisted. Grabbing a sweatshirt, she pulled it on over her pajama top.

"Yes, stop sitting around and let's get going," said Sorrel, padding over the airbeds and stopping expectantly by the door, her fluffy tail held high in the air. "Violet's right. There's no time to waste."

Bracken bounded over to her. "For once I agree with you, pussycat," he said, his eyes shining with excitement and his bushy tail wagging. "Let's go!"

3
A Trip to the Clearing

Mia looked around the clearing, worry swirling in her stomach. The trees' branches were bare, and even the evergreen fir trees were losing their pine needles. The grass was brown, the air smelled of dampness and decay, and the stream that usually tumbled and splashed down a series of rocks before flowing into the trees was moving sluggishly.

The clearing was usually such a peaceful, beautiful place, with flowers blooming and birds singing and forest creatures scampering through the undergrowth. Now, it felt eerily quiet and still.

Bracken growled at Mia's side. "Someone has definitely been doing dark magic here."

Sorrel stalked around the clearing. "I agree. The air feels wrong—weaker."

"It smells sour," said Willow, her delicate ears flickering.

"I don't like it," said Juniper, jumping from Lexi's shoulder into her arms, his tail quivering.

"Can you smell Shades?" Violet asked Sorrel.

Sorrel sniffed the air. "No. I think whoever has just been here doing magic has not been conjuring Shades this time."

Shades were evil spirits. They could be conjured from the shadows by people using dark magic. Once in the human world, they caused trouble by encouraging feelings like jealousy, envy, and fear. Only last week, the girls and their animals had found three

Shades trapped in dreamcatchers who had been manipulating people's dreams, making them behave in strange and frightening ways. They had managed to send them back to the shadows—but only just. They hadn't found out who had conjured and trapped the Shades, but they were sure it was the mysterious figure Mia kept seeing making potions in the clearing.

"I didn't see any Shades in my dream," Mia put in. "I just saw a person making a potion."

"Using plant magic," Bracken added.

As well as Star Magic that the girls used, they knew there was crystal magic, which involved using the energy inside crystals, and plant magic, which involved using the properties of plants and the energy inside them to make potions.

Violet started to hunt around. "Let's see if we can find any clues about who she is."

Mia thought back to the dream. In the

center of the clearing, the grass was flattened, but there were no footprints. She looked at the bramble bush growing there and bent down to examine it. It was the bush that the woman had made burst into flowers, she was sure of it. Looking at it, she realized that there was another plant with long, twining tendrils creeping over the top. Her eyes caught a flash of white. Carefully parting the tendrils, she saw a single white and pink flower.

She picked it.

"Look! This is one of the flowers I saw the person using," she called.

"Do you know what type of flower it is?" Sita said, coming over with Violet.

Mia shook her head.

Violet examined it. "I don't either. Lexi!" she called to where Lexi was searching around in the bushes at the edge of the clearing. "Do you know what kind of this flower is? Come over."

"Wait!" Lexi's voice was urgent. "There's something here under this bush. It's a bird. Its wing is injured."

The flower was instantly forgotten. Putting it into her pocket, Mia hurried over with the others. A thrush was under the bush. It was flapping one wing, but the other lay useless on the ground. It started to panic as the girls crowded around.

"Oh, the poor thing," Sita said softly. "Stay back, everyone!"

They all moved away as she crouched down

and gently put her hands around the bird. Its working wing beat frantically, and it pecked at her hands, but she didn't flinch. "Shhh," she soothed it. "I can help you."

The fear faded from the bird's eyes, and it relaxed. Mia realized Sita must be using her calming magic. Sita picked it up, gently untangling it from the brambles. The others stayed still, not wanting to scare it again.

"Its wing is broken in three places," Sita said, putting the bird on her knee and rubbing its brown feathers.

"How do you know?" Violet asked.

"I just do," Sita said simply. "It's part of my magic."

"Can you heal it?" Mia asked anxiously.

"I can try," Sita said, biting her lip. "But I've never healed a broken bone before—let alone three."

"I think it might take a lot of power to heal broken bones," said Sorrel.

"Just try, Sita," Willow urged her. "I'm sure you can do it."

Sita took a deep breath and closed her eyes, opening herself to the current. Mia knew she would be feeling the magic sparkling and fizzing inside her. Sita placed her hand gently on the bird's wing. The others waited as the seconds passed.

After what felt like forever but was really less than half a minute, Sita opened her eyes. "I can't do it," she said, her shoulders sagging with disappointment. "I can take the pain away, and I can feel the bones shifting back to where they should be, but I can't make them stay in place."

"What are we going to do?" said Lexi.

"Maybe we should take it to a vet," said Violet.

Sita nodded. "I'm sorry," she whispered unhappily to the bird. "I really want to help you, but I can't." She moved as if to stand.

"Wait," Sorrel said suddenly. "Let's think about this. Maybe if you all work together, you can help Sita."

"What do you mean?" Bracken said. "The others can't do healing magic."

"No, but they can draw on the magic current—if they all do that while touching Sita, they might be able to give her extra power."

"It could work," said Juniper, flicking his bushy tail in excitement.

"What do you think?" Mia said to Bracken.

"I think you should try," he urged. "Star Friends are supposed to work together. Sorrel's idea is a good one."

"Of course it is, Fox!" said Sorrel smugly. "I wouldn't have a bad idea, would I?

Now, are you going to try, girls, or just sit around talking?"

Mia sighed. Sorrel and Violet could be so alike—both annoying at times, but both extremely clever, brave, and loyal.

The girls moved closer to Sita and put their hands on her. Mia felt the magic current surge inside her. It swirled around her body as it usually did, making her feel as if her blood were tingling, but instead of staying inside her, she felt it flow through her hand and out into Sita. A feeling of being one with the whole world filled her.

"It's working!" Sita breathed after a few moments. "I can feel the magic power, and now the bones are mending. They're fusing together. That's it!" she gasped. They all opened their eyes and saw the bird stretch both wings out and flap them. "We did it!"

The thrush opened its beak and chirped gratefully. Sita got to her feet and gently threw it into the air. It flew off, singing as it went.

Delight rushed through Mia. "It worked!" The animals leaped around happily, and the girls hugged each other.

"Thank you! Thank you for helping me!" Sita said. "It felt amazing!"

"It really did," said Lexi, her hazel eyes shining.

"It was like being swept away by magic," said Mia.

"And look—look at the clearing," said Violet.

They all followed her gaze.

The stream was flowing more quickly now, and the air smelled sweeter.

"Green buds!" Lexi said, running to a nearby tree and pointing to a few small buds that had appeared on its bare branches. "And spring flowers!" she said to a patch of daffodil shoots suddenly pushing up through the soil. "What's happening?"

"Isn't it obvious?" said Sorrel.

They looked at her blankly.

Sorrel sighed. "You all know that when you use magic to do good, it strengthens the

magic current," she explained. "By working together to heal the bird's wing, you did some very powerful magic, and that strengthened the magic current. It's now repairing some of the damage here."

"So the more good we do, the greener the clearing will get?" said Mia.

"Exactly," said Sorrel.

"Will that work even if we're not here in the clearing when we're doing good?" said Violet.

Sorrel nodded. "It's using your magic to do good that counts, not where you do it."

"Then we should all do a bunch of good deeds with our magic!" Violet said.

"As many as possible," Bracken said.

"We can do that!" said Mia in delight.

Lexi beamed. "Good deeds, here we come!"

Willow stepped forward shyly. "Um … wait, everyone." They all looked at her. "Doing good will help, but the only way you can heal the clearing is by stopping the person who is coming here to do dark magic. If you don't, she'll just keep taking the power from the trees to make her horrible potions and conjure Shades."

There was a pause as her words sank in.

"Willow's right," Sita said heavily. "We have to find out who this person is and stop her."

"As soon as possible," Violet agreed.

"But how do we find out who she is?" said Lexi. "Mia tried to see her with her magic but didn't get anywhere."

"I can never see her face," said Mia. "She must be using some kind of blocking spell so she can't be identified with magic."

"So, what do we do?" said Sita.

Just then, Violet's phone rang. "It's Mom," she said, checking the screen. She answered it. "Hi, Mom.... Yes, we're fine, just out for a walk.... Okay. See you soon."

She ended the call. "Mom was checking that we're okay. She's making pancakes for breakfast."

"Yum," said Mia, her tummy rumbling at the thought. "Maybe we'll think of a plan while we're having breakfast."

Lexi grinned. "I definitely think we should try those pancakes and see!"

4

A PLAN

The animals vanished as the girls left the clearing. The overgrown footpath led from the clearing, back through the trees to a road. Lexi lived at the top of it, near the main street.

As they stepped onto the road, Mia glanced at the little house on the other side and felt her heart twinge. It had belonged to her grandma before she died the previous summer. Now, a new family lived there. A black cat was sitting on the front doorstep. It watched them with unblinking green eyes.

"Hey, Lexi!" One of the downstairs windows opened, and a very pretty girl with blond hair looked out.

"Hi, Lizzie!" Lexi called, going over. She was good friends with Lizzie, who had started at their school a few weeks ago. She was in fifth grade, just like them, but the others didn't like her very much. Violet thought she was shallow because she only seemed interested in talking about boys, fashion, and makeup. Mia didn't like her because she had heard her saying mean things about Sita. Sita didn't mind her—she liked everyone—but Lizzie made no secret of the fact that she had no time for Sita, who wasn't interested in fashion and often wore her sister's hand-me-down clothes.

"What are you doing out so early?" Lizzie asked as Lexi went over to the little fence outside the house.

"Oh, we were having a sleepover at Violet's and woke up early, so we went for a walk."

Lizzie's eyebrows rose. "You slept over at Violet's?"

Lexi blushed slightly. "Yeah." She knew her two friendship groups didn't get along.

"Why shouldn't she?" Violet challenged.

Lizzie acted as if Violet hadn't even spoken. "Well, just remember you're coming over later with the rest of the squad, Lexi." She giggled. "And guess what? I sent a message to Tyler, Brad, and Jake last night, and they're coming over, too! But not until five o'clock, so that will give us an hour to do our makeup and hair before they get here."

Lexi grinned. "Sounds fun! See you later."

"Yeah, later!" Lizzie ducked inside and shut the window.

"Sounds *fun*?" Violet echoed as Lexi rejoined them. "Spending an hour doing your hair and makeup and then hanging around with Brad, Tyler, and Jake? Seriously? What exactly is fun about *that*?"

Lexi looked defensive. "I like that kind of stuff."

Mia elbowed Violet. The week before, they had had a big falling-out with Lexi over her friendship with Lizzie, and ever since then, Mia had been trying to accept that Lexi liked Lizzie and her "squad." "Lexi can hang around with them if she wants," she said quickly, slipping an arm through Lexi's. "Just as long as you're always best friends with us," she told her.

Lexi gave her a grateful look. "Always. You know you're my best friends, and the stuff we do together will always come first, but I do like having fun with Lizzie and the others, too."

Violet sighed. "I just don't get it. I really don't. You're clever, Lexi. Almost as—"

Mia stepped on her foot before she could say "as clever as me" and start an argument with Lexi. Sometimes, Violet really didn't think before she spoke.

"Race you all back to Violet's house!" Mia said hastily, setting off up the road. "And no cheating by using you-know-what, Lexi!"

"I can beat you even without cheating!" said Lexi as she sprinted past her.

Laughing, the others charged after her, the conversation about Lizzie forgotten.

★★★

Breakfast was delicious—hot chocolate and fresh pancakes with a choice of syrup or chocolate sauce. Violet's mom and dad were in the kitchen, too, so the girls couldn't talk about magic, but as soon as they had helped clear the table, they headed up to Violet's room.

"So, has anyone had any good ideas about

how we can find out who is doing the dark magic in the woods?" said Violet.

"Maybe we could spy on the clearing and wait until she comes back," said Lexi.

"We could, but she might go there at any time, and we'll be at school during the day," said Violet.

"One thing we haven't figured out yet is what she wants the potions for," said Sita. "What's she doing with them?"

"Maybe the flower we found will give us a clue," said Mia. "Alice who owns the *Fairy Tales* store does some plant magic. Why don't we go to the store and ask her if she knows what kind of potions a flower like that might be used in?"

"That's a good idea," said Lexi.

"Alice doesn't know we're Star Friends," Sita reminded them. "And we can't tell her." The girls had learned before how important it was not to tell anyone about the Star Animals.

"No, we can't tell her that we're Star Friends, but she already thinks we believe in magic," said Violet. "We can pretend to be interested in how plants can be used for magic and start the conversation that way."

Mia nodded. "The store isn't open today," she said, "but we could go tomorrow after school."

"I have gymnastics," said Lexi. "But you three go without me. You can ask Alice about the dreamcatchers while you're there."

The dreamcatchers the Shades had been

trapped in had come from Alice's store. Elizabeth, Lizzie's mom, had bought them from there, and Lizzie had innocently given them out as presents. At first, the girls had suspected Alice must have put the Shades in the dreamcatchers, but it had turned out she knew nothing about dark magic—she only used magic a little, and she always used it for good.

Violet nodded. "We should try to find out where they came from. Somehow the person doing dark magic must have gotten a hold of them before Elizabeth bought them."

"Tomorrow then," Mia declared. "We'll go to the store, and we'll find out what we can!"

5
Visiting with a Friend

When Mia got home a little later, she opened the front door and found her dad in the hallway with Alex, her little brother, who was almost two.

"Come on, Alex, get your boots on," he was saying. "We're going to the park to meet Jack."

Alex shook his head. "I want train." His mouth set in a stubborn line. "Not going."

"We'll find your train when we get back," Mr. Greene said, looking exasperated.

"Come on. I said we'd be there in 10 minutes."

"Not going!" Alex sat down on the floor.

Mr. Greene met Mia's eyes.

"Do you want me to look for it?" she offered.

"Thanks, but I've searched everywhere. Come on, Alex. Please."

Leaving Alex shaking his head, Mia hurried up to her room. Shutting the door, she looked into the mirror on her desk and opened herself to the magic current.

"Alex's train," she breathed at the glass.

The shiny surface swirled, and then a picture appeared of a little blue train. Mia frowned, trying to figure out where it was, and then her eyes widened. It was buried in Alex's sock drawer!

She jumped to her feet. No wonder her dad hadn't been able to find it! She ran to Alex's room, found the train, and hurried downstairs. Alex was struggling as Mr. Greene tried to get him to stand up. "Want train!" he was shrieking.

"I've got it!" Mia exclaimed, holding the train out. It was like magic. Alex's tears dried instantly. "Train!" he said happily.

"Where did you find it?" Mr. Greene asked Mia.

"In his sock drawer," Mia said. "I remembered I saw him putting stuff in there the other day," she fibbed.

"Phew! Thank you!" Her dad gave her a very grateful look. "Good to go now, Alex?"

"Go park!" Alex said, nodding cheerfully, his tantrum forgotten.

They set off. Mia shut the door behind

them, feeling a warm, happy glow inside. It was wonderful when she could use magic to help people. She stuck her head around the doorway into the living room. Her 15-year-old sister, Cleo, was sitting on the couch and reading a magazine. She was still wearing her pajamas and robe and looked like she had just gotten up. Mia didn't know how she could sleep in so long. Half the day was gone! " Hi," she said, seeing Mia.

"Hi, where's Mom?"

"Upstairs, drying her hair. She has someone coming over for coffee this morning." Cleo yawned.

"Did you just get up?" Mia asked her.

Cleo nodded and looked indignant. "I wanted to stay in bed longer, but Mom wouldn't let me. Hey, do you want a hot chocolate, Mia?"

"Yeah," said Mia.

Cleo grinned. "Get me one, too."

Mia rolled her eyes. "Oh, all right."

"Love you, baby sis." Cleo blew her a kiss.

Shaking her head, Mia went to the kitchen to put the kettle on. She and Cleo got along pretty well most of the time. They were very different—Cleo was really into clothes and makeup and shopping—but she was good at listening when Mia had friendship problems, and she usually gave her good advice.

Mia made the hot chocolate, finishing each mug off with whipped cream from a can, tiny marshmallows, and her favorite extra—a drizzle of chocolate sauce around the rim of the mug to make it even more chocolatey. She took Cleo's mug to her and then went back to the kitchen. The PTSA at school was organizing a rummage sale on Tuesday after school to raise money to buy some new sports equipment, and the students had all been asked to bake something to sell that day. Mia liked baking and planned to make some lemon cupcakes. She started getting the ingredients out when the doorbell rang.

Mia heard her mom come downstairs and open the door. "Oh, hi, Elizabeth. Come in," Mia heard her mom saying.

Mia pricked her ears. Elizabeth—that was Lizzie's mom. The two moms came into the kitchen. Elizabeth was carrying a small plastic bag and was looking as glamorous as ever—she had an expensive-looking poncho around her shoulders, her shoulder-length, pale blond hair was swept back in a low bun, and her skin was glowing with carefully applied makeup.

She and Mia's mom had grown up together in Westport but had lost touch after they finished school, and Elizabeth had moved away to London.

"Hello, Mia," Elizabeth said, smiling at her.

"Hi." Mia smiled back. She had only met Elizabeth a few times—she had her own very successful beauty product business and was often away on business—but whenever Mia met her, she was always friendly.

"Coffee?" Mia's mom asked her.

"Yes, please. Black, no sugar," Elizabeth replied.

Mia started to weigh out her ingredients.

"Are you baking?" Elizabeth asked her.

"Yes, I'm making cupcakes for the PTSA sale," said Mia.

"I'm going to that," said Elizabeth. "I'm going to take some samples of my new anti-aging face cream to give out in return for donations to the PTSA. Speaking of which...." She took a small jar out of the bag she was carrying. "I brought some over for you, Nicky," she said to Mia's mom. She smiled. "Not that I'm saying you need anti-aging products, of course!"

"Oh, I definitely do!" said Mia's mom with feeling. "I have so many wrinkles now. If the cream helps my skin look as good as yours, Elizabeth, I'll certainly be buying it!" She unscrewed the lid and started to rub some into her skin. "It smells wonderful."

"It's very good," Elizabeth said. "It's made from natural herbal ingredients—just like all my products."

Mia's mom poured coffee into mugs. "I really admire you for starting your own business. How did you do it?"

"Well, after school, I didn't have the grades I needed to go to college like you and Anna, so I ended up working in a health-food store and began experimenting with making herbal beauty products. I started off selling them in the store, and soon I had people from other stores asking if they could stock them, too. The business grew from that. I still like to experiment and make products at home, but now I have a team that develops the products for me once I've made the initial batch."

"Well, I'm very envious," said Mia's mom, bringing the coffee over and sitting down with her.

"Envious?" Elizabeth frowned as she took her coffee. "Why would you envy me? You have so much—in addition to your job, you have your children, a happy family life, friends."

"But you have those things, too," Mia's mom said in surprise. "You have those *and* a hugely successful business."

Elizabeth nodded slowly. "Yes. I guess."

"Hey, look what I found the other day," Mia's mom said. "This will make you smile." She rummaged through a pile of papers on the kitchen table and pulled out an old photograph. "It's us when we were 10 on a school trip—that one to the animal sanctuary. Mia, take a look!"

Dusting her hands off, Mia went over to the table.

"Oh my goodness," said Elizabeth.

Mia looked over her mom's shoulder. The colors in the photograph had faded slightly, but she could see a group of 10 year olds, dressed in clothes from the 1980s. "That's you, Mom, isn't it?" she said, pointing to a smiling girl with wavy brown hair, a slightly large chin, and freckles.

"Yes, and that's Anna, Lexi's mom," said Mia's mom, pointing out the small girl next to her who had big, round glasses, a toothy smile, and black hair in two neat braids. "And there's Elizabeth."

Mia looked at a very pretty blond girl at the far end of the line of three friends, her arm around the girl next to her. The three of them were all wearing lipgloss, had their hair in side ponytails, and were wearing matching pink and purple sneakers. Mia knew instantly from their confident smiles that they were the popular girls in the class. "You look just like Lizzie!" she said.

"Lizzie really does look like I did when I was younger, doesn't she?" said Elizabeth with a laugh. "They say the apple doesn't fall far from the tree. School was so much fun! The best time of my life. All those friends, and all the parties in high school."

"I didn't get invited to many parties," Mia's mom said to Mia. "I don't remember school being quite so much fun."

Elizabeth smiled. "It's all changed now, hasn't it? Now you seem to have a lot of friends and are very popular."

Mia's mom smiled and clinked her coffee mug against Elizabeth's. "To happiness and friends!" she declared.

Elizabeth nodded. "To happiness and friends," she repeated thoughtfully.

When Mia was in her pajamas that evening, she called Bracken's name, and the two of them cuddled up under her comforter.

Mia giggled. "Your whiskers tickle."

He sighed happily. "I love being your Star Animal, Mia."

She kissed him. "Do you think that little bit of magic I did to help Alex earlier will have helped the clearing?"

"I'm sure it will. Every time any of you uses magic for good—no matter how small a good deed it is—you will strengthen the magic current, and that will help the clearing."

"I hope the person doesn't go back to the clearing tonight and make it worse again," Mia said. She thought about the images she'd seen. "What do you think she is making the potions for?"

Bracken frowned. "Potions made with dark magic can be used to control people or to make people feel bad feelings like jealousy, anger, and greed. They'll work if they're put into food or if they're dropped on people's skin. We must watch out for anything strange or bad happening." His indigo eyes looked serious. "I don't want anyone to get hurt."

"Me, neither," said Mia. Determination flowed through her. "We won't let that happen. Whoever is making the potions had better watch out—we're on their trail. We're going to find them and stop them, whoever they are!"

6
At School

When Mia got up to have breakfast the next morning, her mom was at the kitchen table, yawning.

"Are you okay, Mom?" Mia said.

"Do I look like I'm okay?" her mom snapped. Then she sighed. "I'm sorry, sweetie. I didn't mean to snap at you. I just really didn't feel like getting up this morning. I hope I'm not coming down with a bug." She yawned again. "I'm going to go back to bed. You're okay to walk in on your own, aren't you? Dad can drop Alex off at playgroup for me later."

"Sure," Mia said. "I'll text Violet and meet up with her on the way there."

"Take some money with you from my purse—you need a new school sweater."

Just then, Cleo came downstairs, pushing her tangled hair back from her face. "Why do we have to get up so early for school? I hate mornings," she moaned.

"Me, too," said Mrs. Greene, and wrapping her robe around her, she went back upstairs.

"I don't," said Mia cheerfully.

Cleo glared at her and shoved some bread in the toaster.

"Do you like my new glasses?" Violet said to Mia when they met up.

"Yeah," Mia said. "They look really good."

A few weeks ago, Violet had been to the optician and found that she needed glasses.

"Do you have to wear them all the time?"

"No, just for reading from the whiteboard, really, but I like them." Violet looked over the top of them at Mia.

"It makes me feel like a teacher. Mia Greene, you are in serious trouble," she said in a mock strict voice. "Stay in at recess."

Mia giggled. "Perfect."

As they arrived at school, Mia pointed to the office. "I have to go to the office and get a school sweater," she told Violet. "I'll see you on the playground."

"It's okay—I'll come with you," said Violet. "After all, you might need protecting from Mrs. Sands."

They exchanged grins. Mrs. Sands, the school receptionist, had started at the school a few weeks ago and always seemed to be in a bad mood.

She was in the school office behind the glass screen. She was about the same age as Mia's mom and was watering the array of plants she kept on the windowsill. Mia thought Mrs. Sands had seen her and waited patiently but she didn't turn around, so a minute or so later, Mia tapped on the glass.

Mrs. Sands glanced at her. "Can't you see I'm busy? You'll have to wait!" she snapped.

"I'm sorry," Mia apologized.

Mrs. Sands finished watering the plants and slowly came over to the girls. "Yes, what is it?"

"I'd like to buy a sweater, please," Mia said.

Mrs. Sands huffed as if Mia had said she wanted to dance on the school roof. "What size?" she asked, stomping over to where the boxes of uniforms were kept.

"Medium, please," said Mia.

Mrs. Sands bent down with a groan and rifled through the box. "Right at the bottom, of course," she grumbled. "Here." She slapped it down on the counter and then winced and touched her back.

"Thanks." Mia paid and took the sweater. Then she and Violet hurried outside and to the playground.

"Mrs. Sands is *so* grumpy!" Mia said.

Violet nodded. "I wish Mrs. Bramley was still secretary." Mrs. Bramley had been really nice.

They spotted Sita and Lexi and ran over to them.

"So, has anyone else done anything good with magic since yesterday?" Sita whispered as they went to a quiet place so they could talk.

Violet nodded. "I shadow-traveled to my grandma's house yesterday to get my mom's purse—she couldn't find it, and I guessed she must have left it there in the afternoon. I told her I found it under the seat in the car."

"I helped Alex." Mia told them about finding Alex's train.

"And I used my magic to stop Arjun from crying last night," Sita said. "He's teething, so he's been crying a lot and not sleeping well." Arjun was her baby brother.

"I did something, too. On the way home from tennis, I climbed up a tree in the park and got a kite down—it had gotten stuck in the branches," Lexi said.

"So, we've all done good deeds!" said Sita.

"Do you think they've helped the clearing?"

"I can find out!" Mia checked that no one was nearby and then pulled out a pocket mirror. "The clearing," she breathed.

An image of the clearing appeared in the glass.

"Does it look any different?" asked Lexi quickly.

Mia smiled and nodded. "The trees have a lot of green buds on them, and the grass is growing again. There are a few more daffodils, too." She looked up. "Our magic is working!"

"Now, all we need is to find out who's doing the dark magic and stop them," said Violet. "I wonder if we'll find anything out when we go to *Fairy Tales* tonight."

The bell rang, and everyone on the playground started to line up. Mia and the others went over to join them—Mia and Violet were in one fifth-grade class, and Sita and Lexi were in the other with Lizzie, who was just arriving.

She was with her dad. Most days she walked to school on her own, but some days her dad came with her. He had a big, bushy black beard and very green eyes, and he rarely spoke.

"See you later, Dad!" Lizzie said. He stood there. She gave him a little push. "You can go home now." He headed back toward the school gates looking as if he couldn't wait to leave. Mia frowned. He was so different from Lizzie's friendly mom.

Lizzie ran to join her friends, Tara and Sadie, who were standing with some of the popular fifth-grade boys—Tyler, Jake, and Brad.

"Hey, guys!" Lizzie twirled her ponytail and smiled at them. "Yesterday was fun, wasn't it? You'll have to come over again."

"Your trampoline is awesome," said Tyler.

"And your parents are awesome to let you order whatever you want for takeout," said Brad. "I'll come over anytime."

"Me, too," said Tara quickly, and Sadie nodded. Lizzie looked smug. Glancing around, she noticed Mia and the others coming over to the lines.

"Violet!" she said. "Oh my goodness! Do you want me to do your hair?"

Violet looked confused and touched her neat braid. "There's nothing wrong with it."

Lizzie raised her eyebrows. "Oh, I think there is," she smirked. Tara and Sadie giggled. Violet opened her mouth, but before she could speak, Lizzic cut in. "You really are going for the geek-chic look today, aren't you? Oh, no, wait, it's definitely more geek than chic, isn't it?"

Violet lifted her chin and met her cool gaze. "Actually, it's one hundred percent geek, Lizzie," she said. "And one hundred percent is exactly what I got on the math test last week. Unlike you—didn't I hear Mr. Neal saying you had to stay in at lunch and redo yours because you failed it?" She raised her own eyebrows and gave her a "*so there*" look.

Tyler snickered.

"Let's go in, guys," Lizzie said sharply. "Come on, Lexi. Or are you going to hang around with these nerds all day?"

Lexi glanced at Mia, Violet, and Sita.

"It's okay, go," Mia told her.

Giving them an apologetic look, Lexi followed Lizzie and her squad inside.

Mia usually liked school, but that day, she just really wanted it to be over so they could go to *Fairy Tales*. At the end of the day, Mrs. Sands shuffled around the playground, handing out paper plates to everyone as they prepared to go home. "Here, take one of these," she said, shoving them into the children's hands. "They're for the PTSA sale tomorrow." Mia looked at her plate. It had a label stuck on it with a rhyme:

Put cupcakes on me—please don't fail.

It's all to raise money at the PTSA sale!

"I don't need one, thank you," said Sita, trying to hand it back to Mrs. Sands. "My grandma has already made a cake, and it's too big for this plate."

"Take it anyway," snapped Mrs. Sands.

When Mrs. Sands moved on, Sita threw it into the recycling bin on the playground.

Across the playground, Lexi was giggling as Lizzie pretended her plate was a hat and then threw it to Tyler.

"Lexi!" Mia called. "We're going now!"

Lexi said good-bye to Lizzie and ran over. "Lizzie's so funny," she said.

"Yeah, hilarious," said Violet dryly.

"She is!" Lexi protested.

Mia didn't want them to argue. "Hey, we'd better go. One of us will call you later and tell you what happens."

"Thanks! I hope you find out something," said Lexi.

"Lexi! We'll be late for gymnastics," her mom called. "Come *on*!"

Lexi hurried off.

"Poor Lexi," said Violet. "We're going to have way more fun." She grinned at the others. "It's shadow-travel time!" she said.

7

Trying to Solve a Mystery

As soon as they got to Violet's house, they ran up to her room and squeezed into a patch of shadows beside Violet's wardrobe.

"Here we go!" Violet said, taking their hands, and Mia felt the world disappear. For a moment, there was gray all around her, and then her feet bumped into the ground.

Mia blinked and looked around the narrow alley. It ran along one side of the *Fairy Tales* store. There were some garbage cans that belonged to the store and cardboard boxes piled next to them. It was a very strange feeling to step into a patch of shadows in one place and arrive in another place a few seconds later.

The doorbell of the store tinkled as they went inside. Mia breathed in the smell of essential oils that wafted from an oil burner behind the counter in the corner. The store was small, but there were shelves filled with models of fairies, dragons, and unicorns, as well as books on magic, herbs to help people have good dreams, and creams to heal bruises. Wind chimes and dreamcatchers hung from the walls and ceiling.

Alice bustled out from the back room. She was in her sixties, with ash blond hair and twinkling blue eyes. She beamed at them. "Well, hello, dears," she greeted them. "No little pussycat with you today?"

The last time they had been in the store, they had taken Sorrel with them to see if she could smell any Shades there.

"No, my cat is home today," said Violet.

"Well, feel free to browse, but remember, dears, look with your eyes and not your hands," Alice said brightly. Mia only just managed to stop herself from rolling her eyes. Alice always spoke to them as if they were about five.

"Actually, we came in because we wanted to ask you something," Violet said. "We found a flower in the woods. You know a lot about plants, and we were wondering if you could tell us what kind of flower it is."

Mia took the flower out of her pocket and showed it to Alice.

Alice frowned. "This is bindweed. I don't understand. You couldn't have found it in the woods at this time of year. It only flowers in the summer."

Sita stepped closer to her. "We need you to help us without worrying and without asking any questions." Mia heard a new note in Sita's voice and knew Sita was using her commanding magic. "You must tell us what you know."

Alice nodded. "Of course I will," she said obediently. "I'll be happy to help."

"Could someone use bindweed to do something magical?" Mia asked.

Alice's mouth tightened. "Not if they wanted to use magic for good. Bindweed smothers other plants, twining around them, suffocating them. It would only be used in potions that would bring unhappiness, potions to control and harm people. If you are doing magic, the herbs you want to use are good herbs like lavender and chamomile, comfrey and rosemary."

"Oh." Mia exchanged worried looks with the others. That didn't sound good. She took the flower from Alice and pocketed it. "Well, thanks."

"I have plenty of books on plant magic if you are interested," said Alice, showing them to a bookshelf. "I know you all believe in magic as much as I do, and magic can be used to do a lot of good."

Mia longed to say, "We know!" She wished she could tell Alice that she and the others were Star Friends with Star Animals, but the last time they told a grown-up—Aunt Carol—it had almost ended in disaster.

Violet started browsing the books. "These look really interesting."

Sita pointed to a metal sign above the books. "What does that mean?" she asked, her voice normal again now that she had stopped using her magic.

Mia read the swirly lilac writing on the sign:

To all magic-doers, this truth be told:

Magic shall return threefold.

Alice smiled. "That's an important rule," she said. "If you do good things with magic, three times the amount of good will come back to you. If you do bad things, then you risk bringing three times the bad power back on yourself."

"It's like...." Mia broke off. She'd been about to say that it was like how doing good things with Star Magic strengthened the magical current.

"Like what?" Alice asked.

"Nothing," Mia said quickly, but catching Violet and Sita's eyes, she was sure they were thinking the same thing.

Alice smiled at them. "The world would be a better place if more people learned how to use magic to do good."

The girls all nodded.

"I'll come back with my mom and buy one of the books," Violet said.

They said good-bye and left the store. The street outside was bustling with people, and they slipped into the quiet alley.

"So, this is bindweed," Mia said, pulling the flower out of her pocket. "And it's used in potions that can control and harm people."

Sita shivered. "You saw the figure in the woods making a potion with it. I wonder who she's planning to use it on."

"We've got to find out more about her," said Violet. She glanced back at the store. "We forgot to ask about the dreamcatchers. We needed to find out if someone could have put the Shades in them before they were sold in the store."

Mia bit her lip. She'd been so busy thinking about the bindweed that she had forgotten all about the dreamcatchers. "We can't go back in now."

"Wait, hang on. We might not need to. Look!" Sita pointed to the pile of cardboard boxes beside the garbage cans. One of them—a medium-sized box—had a picture of a dreamcatcher on it. "It looks like it might be the box that the dreamcatchers came in."

Mia and Violet hurried over. The box had a business name printed on it —Robinsons Home Decoration—and there was an address on it, too:

Rowlings Business Park

Unit 4B

Chicago

Illinois

Violet snapped a picture of the address with her phone. "We could go there using shadow-travel and check it out," she said eagerly.

"We can't just appear in a warehouse," said Sita.

"No. Maybe it would be better if I used my magic to look," said Mia.

"Okay. Do it!" Violet urged.

Mia took out her pocket mirror and said the address on the box. The mirror swirled, and then a picture of a warehouse formed. It looked very normal. "I want to see inside," Mia said to the mirror. The image changed and showed her a warehouse where people were packing different household things into boxes—mirrors, photo frames, dreamcatchers. "It really doesn't seem like the kind of place where magic is going on," Mia said, looking at the others. "It's just a warehouse. And anyway, it's miles away in Illinois. The person doing dark magic lives near here—near enough to get to the woods. She couldn't have put the Shades into the dreamcatchers at a factory in Illinois."

"So how did the Shades get trapped in them?" said Sita.

"Maybe it was Lizzie," Violet said.

"Lizzie!" Mia spluttered.

"Yes. After all, she gave the dreamcatchers to you, Lexi, Tara, and Sadie. Maybe she's the one doing dark magic!"

"But Lizzie's just a normal 10 year old!" Mia protested.

"Like us, you mean?" Violet said, her eyebrows rising. "We do magic. Why not Lizzie?"

Sita shook her head. "It can't be Lizzie, Violet. I know she's not very nice, but she wouldn't do dark magic."

"It really isn't Lizzie," Mia put in. "The person I see in the woods when I use my magic is too tall. It's definitely an adult."

"Hmm. Okay, maybe you're right," Violet said reluctantly. She thought for a moment. "How about Elizabeth, then?"

Mia pictured Lizzie's elegant, friendly mom. "Seriously? Elizabeth?" She simply couldn't imagine her doing dark magic.

"Why would Elizabeth want to hurt Mia and the others?" Sita said.

"It doesn't make any sense," Mia said to Violet.

Violet heaved a sigh. "Okay, I guess not."

They stared at each other. They'd had high hopes of going to *Fairy Tales* and finding out more, but they didn't seem to be any closer to solving the mystery.

8
An Idea

Mia's dreams contained a jumble of images that night—the school gates; Grandma Anne's house; a silver bottle; the cloaked figure standing in the clearing; a tornado of pine needles. She also heard a laugh echoing around her. She knew it was a laugh she recognized, but she couldn't figure out whose laugh it was.

She woke early. "Bad dreams?" Bracken said to her, cuddling closer.

"Mm-hmm. It's just so frustrating," Mia said. "I feel like I know the person."

Bracken licked her nose. "We'll find out who she is soon, I'm sure."

Mia thought about the potion she had seen the person making and remembered what Alice had said about bindweed being used in potions to control people. She hoped they found out soon enough—before someone got hurt.

When she eventually got up, she found her mom and Cleo both sitting at the kitchen table, yawning, while her dad was getting Alex some breakfast and Alex was drawing a picture with crayons.

Cleo was examining her face in a small mirror. "I have a spot coming on my chin," she grumbled.

"Can I use that?" Mia's mom took the mirror from her and examined her face. "My wrinkles are looking better. That cream of Elizabeth's really does work. I might get some more at the school rummage sale today." She rubbed her eyes. "I just wish I didn't feel so tired."

"Can we just stay at home and have a pajama day today?" said Cleo. "I don't want to go to school."

"It's seriously tempting," agreed her mom. "I don't want to get dressed and go out."

"Mommy, look!" said Alex, waving his picture.

"Not now, Alex," Mom said, pushing the picture away. "I'm really not in the mood."

Mia saw Alex's face fall. "Let me see, Alex. It's beautiful," she said as he showed her his scribbles. "Great job." She gave her mom a sideways look. It wasn't like her to be so grumpy in the morning. "Are you still not feeling very well?"

"I felt fine by bedtime last night," her mom said. "I'm just so tired this morning.

I don't know why."

"Here. Drink this," Mia's dad, putting a coffee down in front of her.

"Thanks," Mom sighed.

Mia got her own lunch ready. "I'll walk to school by myself again today," she said to her mom as she put her shoes and coat on. Her mom was still in her pajamas.

"Okay. I'll see you at the sale after school," Mom said gratefully. "'Bye, sweetie."

"I've got to talk to you!" Lexi hissed as they all met up at recess. "Quick, let's go to the wall where it's quiet. I have an idea."

They headed for the quietest part of the playground. Lizzie was standing with Tara and Sadie, and she called out to Lexi as they passed. "Hey, Lex! Where are you going? My mom bought me some new makeup in London the other day. Aren't you going to come and see it?"

"I'll see it later," Lexi called back.

Lizzie pursed her lips. "I might not want to show it to you later," she said.

"Oh, dear. It looks like poor *Lex* will miss out, then," Violet said dryly. "How will she cope?"

Tara and Sadie giggled. Lizzie swung around to them, and their smiles faded instantly. "Come on. Let's go somewhere else. There's a funny smell over here," she said, putting her nose in the air.

"It must be all that perfume she's wearing," Violet commented to Mia.

Lizzie glared at Violet as Mia giggled.

They walked off to the wall.

"So, what's your idea?" Sita said to Lexi.

"Okay. I've been thinking and thinking about who can be doing the dark magic, and I think it might be Mrs. Sands, the school secretary!" whispered Lexi.

They all stared at her. "Mrs. Sands?" Mia echoed.

Lexi nodded. "Think about it. She started at the school about the same time that the dark magic started. She's really mean, and she's crazy about plants. I went into the office earlier, and she was talking to them!"

For a moment, they all digested the information. "She *is* about the same height as the person I've seen with my magic," Mia said slowly. "And she does have blond hair." She remembered something from her dreams the night before. "And I saw the school gates in my dreams last night. Maybe that's a clue that it's someone from school. Maybe it *is* Mrs. Sands!"

"It's pretty odd that she's taken a job at a school when she obviously doesn't like children very much," said Violet thoughtfully.

"I think we should spy on her," said Lexi.

"Good plan. I'll try to watch her with my magic tonight when she's at home," said Mia, feeling excited.

Violet frowned. "Hang on. How did Mrs. Sands put the Shades in the dreamcatchers that Elizabeth bought?"

"I don't know," Lexi admitted. "I haven't figured that out yet."

"Okay, well, for now, she's our number-one suspect," said Violet. "And we're going to be watching her like hawks!"

When Miss Harris wanted someone to pick up some forms for a school trip from the office, Mia volunteered, hoping she could spy on Mrs. Sands. Mrs. Sands's desk was covered with paper plates filled with cupcakes, and there were more in a big box on the floor. She was writing prices on the plates. "What do you want?" she snapped when Mia knocked.

Mia explained.

"Miss Harris should have picked them up earlier. Here." Mrs. Sands shoved a pile of papers into Mia's hands. "Now get out. Go on! I have enough to do, organizing the pricing of all these cupcakes for the sale this afternoon. All this bending and lifting is no good for my back."

Mia left, taking one last look at the array of plants growing on the windowsill. Could Lexi be right? Could Mrs. Sands really be the person doing dark magic?

The rummage sale was very busy after school. A lot of parents, grandparents, and babysitters came. Mia's mom and dad were both there with Alex. There was a booth selling homemade greetings cards, another selling flower bulbs, a second-hand toy and clothes booth, and one of the parents had set up a bouncy castle for the children to play in. Elizabeth was giving out samples of her face cream, although Lizzie had felt sick at lunchtime and had to go home with her dad.

"Come and try some," Elizabeth called out as Sita's nana passed by.

"Oh, no, no, thank you, not for me," she chuckled. "I'm quite happy with my wrinkles."

"I'll take another jar," said Mia's mom.

"It's good stuff, isn't it? Even if I say so myself," said Elizabeth. "You should try some, David," she said to Mia's dad with a smile. She offered him an open sample jar to try from.

"Are you trying to say I look old, Elizabeth?" he said, pretending to look offended. He rubbed some on his face. "Oh, yes, I can feel the years simply dropping away!" he chuckled.

"I'm sorry about him," Mia's mom said to Elizabeth. "I'll move him on before he drives other customers away!" Linking arms with him, she pulled him across the playground. Mia, who had watched the exchange, saw Elizabeth staring after them, her eyes narrowing. But then Lexi's mom walked up to the table, and Elizabeth's face relaxed into a smile of greeting, making

Mia think she must have imagined it.

"Let's go and buy some cupcakes," said Sita. "I'm hungry."

They went over to the cupcake table. Mrs. Sands was supervising with some of the parents from the PTSA. The cupcakes all looked really yummy. As they were choosing one each, Violet squeaked. "What is it?" Lexi said, looking at her.

"I'll tell you in a minute!" Violet whispered, her face pale.

As soon as they had paid for their cupcakes, they hurried away from the table.

"Don't eat it!" Violet said, swiping the chocolate cupcake out of Mia's hand just as she was about to take a bite of it.

"What? Why?" Mia said in astonishment.

"Don't you see?" Violet said. "Mrs. Sands has been in charge of the cupcakes all day! She could have easily slipped something into them—a few drops of a dangerous potion on the top of each cupcake...." They all looked at their cupcakes, and Mia felt her appetite fade.

"You mean she could have poisoned the cupcakes?" she whispered, glancing over at sour-faced Mrs. Sands.

"Well, probably not poisoned, but put some kind of bad magic inside them," said Violet.

Sita stared around the playground. "But everyone is eating them! What's going to happen?"

Mia felt a chill sweep through her.

"What should we do?" said Sita.

Mia bit her lip. What she wanted to do was jump up and down and yell at everyone not to eat the cupcakes, but she would get into so much trouble if she did that. For starters, they had no evidence—no proof that there was something wrong with them. "I guess we just watch and see what happens," she said anxiously.

Sita gulped. "I really hope everyone's going to be all right."

9
STRANGE HAPPENINGS

Mia and the others watched the playground anxiously, but to their relief, no one started behaving strangely.

"Maybe the cupcakes were okay after all," Mia said to Bracken when she got home.

"Maybe, but it does sound like this Mrs. Sands might be the kind of person to do dark magic, though," said Bracken. "Can you spy on her?"

Mia nodded and took her mirror from her pocket. Sitting cross-legged on her bed, she whispered Mrs. Sands's name and held her breath. Would the magic show her anything? If it just showed her darkness, then that might mean Mrs. Sands was blocking anyone from spying on her with magic, and that would be a sure sign that she was guilty.

However, a picture formed. It showed Mrs. Sands sitting on her couch at home watching TV. A man, whom Mia guessed must be her husband, was sitting in a chair. It all looked very normal. Mia scanned the room. There were plenty of plants in pots, but absolutely nothing else unusual. *But Aunt Carol's house looked normal*, she reminded herself. *Maybe Mrs. Sands has a secret room somewhere where she does dark magic, just like Aunt Carol had in her basement.*

As she watched, Mrs. Sands rubbed her back and winced.

"How's it feeling?" her husband asked.

"Really bad today," she said.

"You need to go to the doctor again," he said. "You can't go on like this."

She nodded. "I will. I'll go for a little walk later and see if that helps make it feel better."

It wasn't exactly an interesting conversation to listen in on. Mia spoke to the mirror. "Show me *all* the other rooms in the house," she said.

The picture changed. She saw a kitchen, a dining room, a hallway—all looked normal. A master bedroom, a spare bedroom, a bathroom. There was nothing unusual at all.

"Show me the yard," she said.

It was dusk outside, but the mirror showed her a beautifully kept flower garden with neat flowerbeds filled with spring bulbs. A figure moved in the shadows near the living-room window. Mia caught her breath as she recognized her. Violet! Another movement caught her eyes. She had Sorrel with her, too!

"What is it?" Bracken asked, seeing her face.

"Violet and Sorrel are there. They must have shadow-traveled to the yard," Mia told him. She watched Violet creep through the shadows and peek in through the window. It was such a Violet thing to do—just to go without discussing it with the rest of them. "I hope she doesn't get caught! And anyway, there's nothing for her to see there. I took a look at the whole house." She put the mirror down and pulled out her phone. She texted Violet.

I know where u are! I can c u. But u can go home. I've checked it out already. It's normal. Go home! Don't get caught!!!!

She picked up the mirror again and watched as Violet took her phone out and read her message. Violet grinned as she read it and then waved as if knowing Mia could see her. The next moment, she and Sorrel vanished.

Mia looked up at Bracken. "They went home."

Just then her dad called up the stairs. "Dinnertime, Mia."

"I'd better go," said Mia, putting her mirror down. "I'll come back as soon as I can."

By the time Mia had finished dinner, there was a text message waiting for her from Violet.

So it's not Mrs. S then?

Mia sat down on the bed and replied.

I dunno. I didn't c anything suspicious. But it still cd be I guess.

She called Bracken. He appeared and jumped onto her knee. "What now?" he said, licking her face.

"I'm not sure," she admitted.

Her phone buzzed.

Mia! I'm in the woods, and the person just went past me and into the clearing! Sorrel won't let me stay and spy. She says it's too dangerous on my own. Can u take a look? Xx

Mia quickly told Bracken what it said and replied.

Get out of there. I'll tell u what I see. Xx

She grabbed her mirror. "Bracken! Mrs. Sands said she would go for a walk later. Maybe she *is* the person doing dark magic!" She held the mirror close. "Show me the clearing!"

A picture appeared. It showed the familiar figure in the dark cloak standing in the clearing using a potion to draw a circle of green light around herself. Mia frowned. Could it be Mrs. Sands? She was about the right height. Mrs. Sands had blond hair, and once in the past, Mia had seen a strand of blond hair fall across the figure's face.

"Go as close as you can," she told the mirror.

The image of the person grew larger and larger, like a camera zooming in. As she finished the circle, the trees and plants around the clearing started to tremble and shake. The figure stiffened and straightened up at once. She spun around, staring. "Spy!" she exclaimed wildly. Mia's heart skipped a beat. Somehow the person had realized she was being watched! "Who are you? Where are you?"

Mia gasped and cut off the magic flow. The image vanished. Mia's heart pounded as she lowered the mirror to her lap.

"What is it?" Bracken asked.

"I saw her, but then she realized someone was watching her," Mia said uneasily. "I don't know how, but she just knew."

"She must be using some kind of warning spell to alert her if someone is spying on her," said Bracken.

Mia didn't feel like doing any more magic after that. When she went to sleep, she hugged Bracken tightly. But during the night, she had a horrible dream. She saw two eyes peering through blackness, glowing green like a cat's eyes. The spooky eyes swept from side to side and then seemed to fix on Mia. "*You!*" hissed a voice Mia was sure she knew.

Mia sat up, her heart racing in her chest. Bracken was awake instantly. "What is it?" he asked. "What did you dream about?"

She told him.

He looked worried. "We have to tell the others about this. It sounds like the person might know who you are now!"

Mia took a shaky breath and tried to be brave. "Maybe that's a good thing. We want to find out who she is, after all. Maybe if she comes after me, that'll help us catch her."

Bracken nodded slowly, but Mia could see the concern in his eyes.

The girls went to Violet's house after school. Lexi wasn't sure her mom would let her miss her piano lesson, and she took the others with her to where her mom was standing with Mia's mom to help persuade her. To her astonishment, her mom seemed okay with the idea.

"Sure, whatever," Lexi's mom said, waving her hand in the air. "It's no big deal if you miss one lesson. You go and hang out with your friends tonight. Nicky and I are going to the Copper Kettle for a coffee."

"Thanks, Mom," said Lexi, giving the others a surprised look.

Mia's mom linked arms with Lexi's mom and gave her a nudge. "After that, we could play some pool before dinner."

It was Mia's turn to feel astonished. Her mom hardly ever went out to play pool.

Lexi's mom giggled. "Sure, why not?" she replied.

"We'll see you guys later!" Lexi's mom said to the girls.

"*You guys?*" Lexi whispered to the others as they hurried away. "Did you hear that? My mom never says *guys*."

"My mom is acting weird, too," said Mia. "I can't believe she said she wanted to go play pool!"

She spotted her dad standing with a group of other dads near where Alex was playing on the jungle gym. A couple of them were playing air guitars. "See you at home later, Mia!" her dad called. "I'm going to go and grab my guitar and have a jamming session with the boys. Get yourself some dinner if Mom and I aren't home."

Mia frowned. "What's going on?" she said to the others. "My dad hasn't played his guitar in years." She shook her head. "I don't like this. When the adults start behaving strangely, it usually means dark magic is going on."

"The cupcakes must have had potion in them after all!" said Lexi.

"Mr. Neal was a little weird today," said Sita. "We were supposed to be having a math test, but he let us do art all afternoon, and we were allowed to listen to the radio, and then he pretended to drum along to some of the songs on his desk!"

"Yeah." Violet nodded. "We were supposed to have a math test, too, but we didn't. We just played math games and read instead while Miss Harris kept checking her phone."

"There *must* have been something in the cupcakes!" said Lexi, shooting a look at where Mrs. Sands could be seen sitting in the school office. "We were right!"

"But it's just adults who are being weird, not children, so it can't be the cupcakes because everyone ate them," Violet argued. She shook her head. "This is all so confusing. I know what we should do. I think we should go to the clearing tonight—all of us together—and hide and see if the person comes. Then if she does, we'll try to see her face."

The others gave her dubious looks. "It's the perfect opportunity," she told them.

"Whatever's going on with the adults is stopping them from worrying about us and where we are, so let's make the most of it."

Lexi frowned. "But what if she sees us?"

"Sita can command her to freeze," said Violet. "Look, Mia might be in danger if this person knows who she is. We can't just ignore that. We have to do something, and this is the best plan."

Lexi and Sita didn't look too sure, but Mia nodded. She'd felt uneasy all day, as if she might be attacked at any minute. She couldn't go on like this. "Let's do it!" she said.

10
Danger in the Clearing

The girls dumped their bags at Violet's house and walked down the street to the clearing. As they passed Lizzie's house, they heard old pop music. They glimpsed a figure dancing through the window. "Looks like Elizabeth's been affected like the other adults," said Violet. She paused. "No, wait. That's Lizzie!"

Lexi frowned. "Lizzie wouldn't be dancing to 1980s music."

But they could clearly see Lizzie dancing and singing along, blond ponytail swinging.

Violet grinned. "Who'd have thought she would turn out to have a thing for pop music? Even I know that's not exactly cool."

Lizzie's black cat was sitting on the doorstep. It watched them with unblinking green eyes as they crossed the street and headed down the path that led to the clearing.

As soon as they got there, they called their animals' names. Bracken, Sorrel, Juniper, and Willow appeared. They were delighted to see the girls. Juniper scampered up to Lexi's shoulder and rubbed his cheek against her face. Sorrel twined around Violet's legs, while Willow butted Sita gently with her head and Bracken put his paws up on Mia's knees. She crouched down and hugged him.

"We're all together," Willow said happily.

"So much has been happening," said Sita. "We have a lot to tell you." They sat down on some tree trunks and told the animals about Mia's dream, about the strange way the adults were behaving, and then Violet told them about her plan.

"I wanted to stay last night and try to see the person's face to know if it really was Mrs. Sands, but Sorrel wouldn't let me."

"It was much too dangerous to be here on your own," said Sorrel. "Even for someone with your powers, Violet." She rubbed her cheek against Violet's arm.

Willow nodded. "Whoever we're dealing with is capable of extremely powerful magic. She could attack you and really hurt you."

"I've got an idea!" Juniper bobbed up and down on Lexi's shoulder. "Why don't you all try to use the magic current to create barriers to protect you from dark magic?"

"Like invisible shields, you mean?" said Bracken.

"Yes," said Juniper, his tufty ears twitching. "When we were in the Star World, I heard that some humans can use the magical current to make defensive barriers."

"It's not a bad idea," said Sorrel, flicking her tail around her paws. "It would certainly help protect you if it works. Give it a try."

"What do we do?" said Mia uncertainly.

"Connect to the magical current, but instead of using it to do the things you normally do, imagine it protecting you," said Sorrel.

Mia breathed in and let the magic current flow into her. It was like turning a switch on inside her. When she connected to the magic current, she felt as if sparkles were flowing through her. Her body tingled, and she felt somehow as if she were linked to nature. She imagined a barrier surrounding her, an invisible shield that would protect her no matter what. She saw the air shimmer, and a large bubble formed around her. "I think I did it!" she said to Bracken, who was sitting at her feet and was in the bubble, too. "I've done something, anyway. Look!"

"Great job, Mia!" said Bracken, jumping up. "I wonder if it'll protect you."

Mia glanced at the others. None of them had a bubble around them.

Sita noticed Mia's shield. "Look at Mia!" she exclaimed.

Mia tried to concentrate on staying connected to the magical current. She knew that if she got distracted, then the shield would disappear. "See if it works!" she told them.

Lexi chucked a pine cone at Mia. It hit the

magic bubble and bounced back.

Violet cheered. "It does work! Go, Mia!"

Mia grinned. She was used to Sita and Violet having all the extra powers. It felt good to be able to do something special herself.

Lexi picked up a branch and threw that, but the same thing happened.

"Let me try!" said Willow. She charged at the bubble with her head down, but as she hit it, she bounced off and landed in a heap on the ground. She shook herself and got to her feet. "It's a really good barrier, Mia!"

"Now we just need to do it, too," said Lexi. "How did you do it, Mia?"

Mia explained, and the others tried again. Lexi managed to create a weak bubble, but it burst when Mia threw a pine cone at it.

Violet and Sita couldn't make a bubble at all, no matter how hard they tried. Mia tried to help them, but it was no good.

"I just can't do it," said Violet in frustration. She glanced at the darkening sky. "We should stop trying now and hide in case the person comes along."

"Where should we hide?" said Sita, looking nervous.

"In the trees, close to the footpath but far enough back so that she won't see us," said Mia.

The others nodded. They pushed their way into the trees, their clothes snagging on brambles. They could see the footpath to the left of them.

"Everyone stay very still and quiet," Willow whispered.

"And no rushing into the clearing when we see her," said Lexi, looking warningly at Violet.

"No, it's too dangerous," agreed Juniper. "Just try to see her face, and then we can decide what to do afterward."

They all nodded. Sorrel stiffened. "I can hear someone coming!"

"This is it!" whispered Violet, her eyes shining with excitement. "We're finally going to find out who she is!"

They crouched down in the shadows, hardly daring to breathe. Mia's heart was banging so loudly in her chest that she was sure everyone else would be able to hear it, too. She hoped no one coughed or sneezed!

A cloaked figure came striding along the footpath. It was so strange to see the figure in real life after seeing her with magic for so long. Mia's hands grew sweaty with anticipation. They might see her face at any moment!

The person walked to the middle of the clearing and pulled out a small brown bottle. She began to use the liquid inside it to draw a green circle around herself, but her hood kept her face hidden.

As the last drop joined up with the first, the trees around the clearing started to tremble. The person straightened up with a start and glared around, the large hood still hiding her face. The trees shook more violently.

"*Spies!*" the woman hissed, and she swept

her arm around the clearing. A green light flashed in front of the girls, revealing their hiding place. They all blinked in the bright light, illuminated like deer in headlights on a road.

"You four!" The person pointed at them, and almost before they knew what was happening, the plants around them exploded. Brambles, thorny branches, and ivy twined around them and their animals. Tree branches swept down toward them, aiming for their faces. Sita screamed in fear, Violet yelled, and Lexi grabbed Mia and pulled her down out of the way of a branch about to hit her head. Mia had no time to think about creating a magical barrier because she was too busy ducking and dodging the branches to be able to focus. She shouted out as a creeper wrapped around her legs, knocking her over. She thudded into the damp, leafy ground and felt the creeper tighten around her.

Bracken snarled furiously and bit through the creeper, freeing her. Juniper was gnawing frantically through brambles that had attached themselves to Lexi's wrists. Sorrel clawed at the ivy that was snaking over the girls' shoes. Lexi jumped to her feet and leaped around, using her agility and speed to grab the tree branches before they hit the others.

"We've got to get out of here!" Violet cried.

"Go!" yowled Sorrel.

Violet grabbed Mia and Sita's hands. "Run, Lexi! I'll bring Sita and Mia!"

"Got it!" cried Lexi.

Violet's fingers tightened on Mia's, and Mia felt the world disappear. There was a brief moment where everything was gray, and then her feet hit carpet, and she blinked and found herself in Violet's bedroom. There were twigs in her hair, and her face and arms were scratched and bleeding. The others looked just as bad. They all collapsed onto the carpet, panting.

"Bracken!" Mia gasped quickly. He appeared beside her, his coat matted with burrs and long brambles trailing from his bushy tail. Mia felt a rush of relief. The others called their animals, too.

"That was so close," said Lexi shakily as Juniper leaped into her arms.

Willow and Sorrel pressed close to Sita and Violet. Willow was trembling, and even Sorrel looked ruffled.

Mia buried her face in Bracken's fur. "I couldn't create a magic barrier," she said. "I'm sorry. There was just too much going on."

"Don't worry. I couldn't get the words out to command anyone or anything," said Sita. "It was so scary."

"She knew us!" said Violet grimly. "Whoever it was recognized us. Did you hear what she said? *You four.* That means she knows us. I bet it *was* Mrs. Sands! I wish we'd seen her face."

Mia frowned. Although she agreed that a lot of the evidence pointed to it being Mrs. Sands, there was something telling her the person in the woods wasn't the school secretary. Something that didn't fit. What was it? Her voice, maybe? No, it was something else.

"We didn't see her face," said Sita.

"Well, whoever it is knows who we are now and knows we're Star Friends," said Violet.

An image of Aunt Carol filled Mia's mind. When she had found out that they were Star Friends, she had almost managed to trap their animals and remove the memory of magic from Mia's mind. She looked around at her disheveled friends, a feeling of foreboding shivering down her spine. This wasn't good. It wasn't good at all.

11
Trapped!

Sita healed everyone's cuts and scratches, and then they all went home. Mia got back to find her parents were still acting strangely. Her dad was playing video games, and her mom was doing her nails with Cleo and letting Alex have chips and cookies for dinner.

Mia made a sandwich for him and for herself, and then she got him into his pajamas and put him to bed. She didn't want to have to try to figure anything else out that night. Whatever was going on with her parents, they

seemed happy enough. She would deal with them another time. Right now, she was more worried about herself and the others.

She wasn't looking forward to going to sleep in case those eyes appeared in her dreams again. She hugged Bracken until she drifted off.

To her relief, the eyes didn't appear, although a succession of images flashed through her mind, many the same as before: the school gates … the silver bottle … pine needles swirling in a storm … trees shaking … ivy shaking and rustling….

She became aware of Bracken licking her face. "Mia! Wake up!" he repeated urgently. She looked at him, realizing that the rustling she had heard in her dreams hadn't stopped.

She sat up. "What's happening?"

Bracken leaped off the bed and raced to her open window. "Look!"

Mia stared. A blanket of ivy was creeping over her windowsill, the tendrils crawling into her room.

She jumped to her feet and slammed the window shut. The ivy writhed as if its tendrils were snakes. She snapped the branches off and they finally stopped moving, but the rest of the ivy continued to rustle as it slithered over the glass outside.

Mia backed away from the window. "What's going on?" she said in alarm.

"It's like it's spying on us," said Bracken.

Mia's phone buzzed. She grabbed it from her desk and saw Lexi had just sent a group message to her and the others.

There's ivy all over my window!

The phone buzzed again, this time with a message from Sita.

Mine, too! What's going on?

Mia typed quickly.

It's on mine, too. Bracken thinks it's spying on us.

Violet joined in, too.

Sorrel thinks that as well. I was about to text u. Sorrel says to try to ignore it. It'll disappear at daybreak. The person is just trying to freak us out.

Lexi's reply came right away.

She's succeeding! U do realize that this means she must know where we all live?!!!

Mia glanced at the time. It was 4:30 a.m. She sat down on her bed and watched the ivy crawl over her window until the sun started to rise. Only then did the ivy disappear, creeping back down the wall, and finally the rustling stopped. Mia slumped back against the pillows and rubbed her eyes with her hands. She was exhausted, and she had no idea what the day was going to hold. She could feel danger closing in on them like a dark, gray cloud. She wanted to stand up to it and fight it, but how could she when she didn't know for sure whom they had to fight?

"I don't like this, Bracken," she said.

"I know," he agreed unhappily. "Neither do I."

When Mia went downstairs for breakfast, she was relieved to find that her dad seemed to be back to normal. He was getting Alex's breakfast and making Mia's lunch.

"Where's Mom?" Mia asked.

"Refusing to get up," said her dad. He shook his head. "She stayed up until about two o'clock last night watching a movie with Cleo. I thought I'd better let her sleep in."

He and Alex walked Mia to school. As they got there, Mia saw Mrs. Sands getting out of her car. Mia frowned. Had the person in the clearing been Mrs. Sands?

No! As she watched Mrs. Sands straightening up gingerly, her hand on her back as if it were hurting, Mia suddenly realized what had been nagging at her. Mrs. Sands always moved slowly, as if she were in pain, and she'd been talking to her husband about her back hurting the other night. The person in the clearing moved easily and stood straight and tall.

It's not Mrs. Sands. The realization beat through Mia. Her heart plummeted. So they were still no closer to figuring out who it was.

Mia hurried onto the playground, hoping the others would be there. She noticed that there were fewer adults than usual there. Many of those who were there were glued to their phones or yawning and looking grumpy. But some looked normal, dressed in their workout clothes or work outfits.

"Hi," Violet said, coming over to her. She had shadows under her eyes and looked as tired as Mia felt.

"Hi," Mia said. "I need to talk to you—and the others." She dropped her voice. "It's not Mrs. Sands."

"Why not?"

"I'll tell you when the others get here."

They headed over to the wall. On the way, they passed Lizzie standing with Tara and Sadie, and Brad, Tyler, and Jake. Lizzie had come into school that day with makeup on—blue eyeshadow, eyeliner, and red lipstick.

"What do you think?" she was saying,

pouting at Tara and Sadie.

"You look really cool!" said Tara.

Lizzie sighed. "Tara, no one says cool anymore."

"Awesome?" Tara tried.

Lizzie sighed even louder. "It's fierce. Okay? Fierce."

"Yeah, okay, Lizzie, you look really fierce," Tara said quickly.

"Fierce!" Violet said, rolling her eyes at Mia.

Lizzie heard and turned to look at her. "You know, I think it's really brave of you, Violet," she said with a fake smile, "the way you just come to school each day not caring what you look like."

"*I'm* brave?" Violet snorted. "I think you're brave coming to school with your face made up to look like a clown!"

The boys all burst out laughing. Lizzie flushed a furious bright red.

"Yeah, blushing makes you look even more like one!" said Violet with a grin.

"You're the worst!" Lizzie spat, and she flounced away.

"Clown face!" chuckled Brad.

"Nice one, Violet," called Jake.

"You really shouldn't wind Lizzie up like that," said Mia as she and Violet went over to the wall. "It just makes her mad."

"So?" said Violet. "I don't care, and neither do you. You don't like her any more than I do."

"No, I don't," Mia admitted. A grin caught at her lips. "And that *was* really funny.

Did you see her face when you said she looked like a clown?"

Violet grinned back. "She was FURIOUS!"

They waved to Lexi and Sita, who were just coming onto the playground. "Mom's still being odd," said Lexi as she and Sita joined them at the wall. "She said I can skip swimming tonight, too. Are we going to meet up?"

"Not in the woods," said Sita with a shiver. "I don't want to be anywhere near ivy or brambles right now."

Mia nodded. She felt the same way. "Let's go to the beach," she said. "We can talk there and decide what we do next. But first I need to tell you something. I don't think you-know-who is Mrs. Sands."

She explained what she'd noticed in the parking lot.

"You're right," Violet said. "She always shuffles around. She doesn't move like the person we saw last night at all."

There was a rustle behind them. Mia looked around sharply. It was just some daffodils in the grass, blowing in the breeze.

After school, they headed toward the beach through the woods.

"What's that?" said Lexi, pointing to something white on the ground by the edge of the forest. She bent down and picked up a flower head. "Bindweed," she said in surprise.

"Bindweed?" echoed Sita with a gulp.

"I bet the person dropped it. She might be in the clearing right now!"

said Violet. "Let's go and see!"

"No!" Lexi gasped, grabbing her arm. "Violet, we can't just go racing into the clearing. You know what happened yesterday!"

"But this time, we'll be ready for her," said Violet. "Sita, the second we see her, you have to use your magic. Tell her to freeze."

"I really don't think this is a good idea," said Lexi.

"I agree with Lexi," said Sita.

"But this could be our chance to stop her!" said Violet. "She's not going to be expecting us, so we can surprise her. Come on!"

"No," said Lexi.

"Well, I'm going!" said Violet, running through the trees.

"Violet!" Mia shouted. But Violet didn't stop. Mia ran after her. She wasn't going to let her go into the clearing alone.

As she followed Violet, she heard a rustle. It came from the trees to the right. She glanced over and saw a cloaked figure there. "Violet! Look!"

Violet had seen. She leaped toward the figure, who started to hurry away. Mia charged after Violet, but as she did so, a little warning voice in her brain was telling her something was wrong. The figure didn't look quite the same as usual. It was taller and broader, and was that black hair poking out from under the hood?

A laugh rang out behind them. Mia and Violet skidded to a halt and looked over their shoulders. A hooded figure appeared behind them. Mia's blood turned to ice. *Two* hooded figures? What was going on?

"It's a trap!" Violet exclaimed.

The figure behind them threw a handful of pine needles into the air. Almost immediately, more pine needles swirled up from the ground and swept around them, whirling faster and faster. Violet and Mia cried out as the needles stabbed at them. They covered their faces with their arms, trying to protect their eyes. As they did so, creepers reared up and wrapped around their legs. Mia tried to kick them off, but they held her tightly. Her heart pounded. They were trapped! What were they going to do now?

12
A Dark Revelation

"Bracken!" Mia yelled at exactly the same time that Violet called Sorrel's name. Bracken and Sorrel appeared instantly. At the same moment, the pine needles suddenly stopped whirling and fell motionless to the ground.

Bracken growled and leaped at one figure while Sorrel sprang toward the other.

"Bind them all!" the figure closest to the path cried.

Creepers wrapped around Sorrel and Bracken. The trees close to the path started to shake.

Mia suddenly realized this was a warning to the figure—that Sita and Lexi must be coming after them. "Si—" she started to shout.

The figure snapped her fingers. A creeper *thwacked* over Mia's mouth, cutting off her warning. Looking around, she saw one cover Violet's mouth, too, and two more wrap around Bracken and Sorrel's muzzles.

Sita and Lexi stepped through the trees, with Willow and Juniper beside them. Their mouths fell open in horror as they saw Mia and Violet and the animals imprisoned by creepers. Lexi used her magic and leaped forward. In a second, she was beside Mia and Violet, trying to free them.

"I comm—" Sita began to say.

The figure hissed a word, and a tree branch swept down. It hit Sita hard, knocking her on the head. She collapsed on the ground, unconscious. Creepers instantly twined around her, covering her mouth.

"Sita!" Mia tried to shout, but all that came out was a muffled sound.

"Bind the rest, too!" ordered the figure, and before Lexi could do anything, creepers snapped over her and Sita's wrists and ankles, and caught Juniper and Willow, too.

The figure laughed. "How predictable. You each acted just as I thought you would. Did you actually think you could stop me with your feeble Star Magic?"

Mia frowned. The voice was frustratingly familiar. Who was it? And what about the other figure—the black-haired one who was now standing so silently?

"You can't bind us!" Sorrel hissed.

The Star Animals vanished to nothing in a swirl of starlight, leaving their creepers in coils on the ground. Mia was glad they had gotten free, but she suddenly felt horribly lonely without Bracken there. Squirming wildly, she managed to pry off the creeper covering her mouth.

"Who are you?" she demanded.

"Do you really not know?" The figure laughed in amusement and shook the hood back, revealing her face, framed by blond, shoulder-length hair.

"Elizabeth!" Mia felt as if she had just had a bucket of cold water tipped over her. Beside her, she heard the others gasp, too.

"Yes, it's me." Elizabeth smiled.

Mia looked at the other figure—the silent, black-haired one. "So who's that?"

"I think you've met my cat." Elizabeth snapped her fingers, and the other figure pushed its hood back, revealing Lizzie's dad.

"Your … your *cat*?" Mia said in confusion, wondering what Elizabeth was talking about.

Elizabeth smirked and snapped her fingers again. In front of Mia's astonished eyes, Lizzie's dad changed shape, shrinking and becoming the family's black-haired, green-eyed cat. It shook itself and stalked toward Elizabeth with a meow.

“I don’t actually have a husband,” said Elizabeth. “I needed one at times, to drop Lizzie off at school and things like that, so I used Oscar, my cat, as a stand-in. Isn’t it amazing what you can do with magic?”

Mia’s head whirled. So that was why Lizzie’s dad had always seemed so odd! He wasn’t human!

Lexi managed to wriggle free from the creeper covering her mouth. “Why?” she burst out. “Why are you doing all this?”

Elizabeth smiled. “Because I can,” she said.

Mia felt warm breath on her ankles and jumped. Glancing down, she saw Bracken. He had managed to sneak back and had crept through the undergrowth to her and now, hidden by the leaves, he was gnawing at the creepers tying her ankles. His indigo eyes silently met Mia's. She didn't dare say a word in case she gave him away. If he could free her, then maybe she could free the others—or attack Elizabeth in some way.

Elizabeth was walking back and forth in front of them. "Do you have any idea how much money you can make with dark magic? I discovered early on that plants have the power to make people look younger. If I take the life force from a plant and make a potion with it, then add just one tiny drop into each batch of face cream, the face cream will really work. It actually can make those wrinkles melt away." She looked around the clearing. "This place—this clearing—contains astonishingly powerful magic. I realized it when I came here for a visit last fall. I decided to move back, and ever since I started using these plants and trees in my products, they have worked better than ever."

She smirked. "Of course, the latest batch of face cream has had some rather amusing side effects that I'll have to iron out before I sell it to the wider public. But it has been fun seeing the parents in Westport revert to being teenagers—*really* becoming younger!"

"So that's what's been going on!" Mia realized. "Everyone who has been using the face cream has not just been looking younger, but they've also been acting younger?"

"Yes. The effect only lasts as long as they use the cream, but it's been amusing to watch. There will be consequences from the meetings that have been missed, the responsibilities that have not been met. Chaos will follow for some time to come. Just like with the dreamcatchers I gave to you two and Tara. They brought their own problems to your families, didn't they?" She chuckled darkly. Mia felt the creeper around her ankles give way, and Bracken started on her wrists.

"But why would you want to cause problems for our families?" Lexi said.

Elizabeth's eyes narrowed. "Your mothers were geeks. They weren't supposed to be the success stories and end up with perfect lives." Her voice grew bitter. "I couldn't believe it when I came back and saw how well they had done for themselves. I wanted to upset them. I was the popular one at school. I was supposed to be happy and successful. Not them."

"But that doesn't make sense. You *are* successful," said Lexi, mystified. "You have your business—even if it's based on dark magic—and you've got. . . ." She looked at the cat. "Well, not a husband, but you have Lizzie. What will she think if she finds out about all of this?"

Elizabeth started to laugh. "Oh, Lexi. You think you're so smart, don't you? You're just like your mom—she always thought she was smarter than everyone else, too. But you're not smart enough. Have you really not realized the truth?" She pulled a small gold bottle out of her pocket and held it up. "Taking the life force from the plants to make anti-aging products may be dark magic, but it's nowhere near as dark as the potion I made and put into this little bottle." She held the bottle up. "This is a real anti-aging potion."

"What do you mean?" said Mia uneasily.

"Watch," Elizabeth said, her blue eyes glittering. She put the bottle to her lips and drank, and in front of their horrified eyes, Elizabeth started to shiver and tremble and change—into *Lizzie*....

13
The Power of Star Magic

"So, what do you think?" Lizzie said, twirling the end of her blond ponytail. Everything about her had changed—her clothes, her hair. "You fell for it."

"You're…you're both Lizzie and Elizabeth?" Mia stammered.

"You got it!" Lizzie smirked. "Now, you have to admit that's clever."

Mia glanced at the others. Their eyes showed the horror she was feeling.

"But why would you want to pretend to be

a 10 year old?" Lexi burst out.

"So I could relive my youth," said Lizzie. "Being at school was the best time of my life, and now I get to do it again with all the money I need and without parents telling me what to do. How perfect is that? No one will be more popular than me." She shot a look at Violet. "Although you have been trying to thwart that. Making the boys laugh at me today." Her eyes hardened. "You'll be sorry."

"You're the one who's going to be sorry!" cried Mia. "We'll tell everyone the truth."

"Like they'd believe you!" scoffed Lizzie. "And anyway, you won't be telling anyone anything. Not after I've used this on you." She pulled a second bottle from her pocket—it was made of silver.

Ice ran down Mia's spine. She had seen that bottle in her vision. It had the bindweed potion inside it.

"One drop of this binding potion on your skin, and you'll have to do as I say. Forever." Lizzie smiled coldly. "I will use it on all of you and stop you from revealing the truth about me."

Mia felt the creepers on her wrist loosen as Bracken silently gnawed at them. *Keep going, Bracken*, she willed him. *I've got to get free!*

She glanced at Lexi and Violet and saw faint movement in the undergrowth beside them. She guessed Juniper and Sorrel were trying to free them, too. Willow was the only animal who couldn't help—she was too big to creep up through the bushes, and she didn't have paws or sharp teeth that were good at gnawing. Mia glanced at Sita, who was still lying unconscious on the ground, and wondered where Willow was.

"So, who should I start with?" said Lizzie, clearly enjoying the moment. "Violet, I think. Just imagine all the ridiculous things I can make you say and do when you're bound to obey me, Violet. Now we'll see who gets laughed at."

Violet's green eyes flashed furiously.

Lizzie started toward Violet when suddenly, a blazing fire appeared in front of her.

"What...." Lizzie staggered back, and then her eyes narrowed as she realized it was just an illusion. "Oh, Violet, did you seriously think that was going to stop me?"

Violet pulled her hands up, showing that the creepers were gone, and ripped the one from her mouth. "No, I didn't think that would, but I hoped Willow might!" she cried. She nodded at the nearby trees. "Go, Willow!"

Willow came galloping out. Her usually

gentle eyes were furious as she charged at Lizzie, butting her as hard as she could with her head. Lizzie cried out in shock. Before she had a chance to use her magic, Lexi was on her feet and grabbing a creeper. She swung through the trees, her feet connecting with Lizzie's shoulders and knocking her over. Lizzie sprawled on the ground just as Mia's bonds finally broke, and she leaped to her feet and raced to Sita with Bracken beside her.

"Sita, wake up!"

Bracken started to lick Sita's face. Willow cantered to her side and nuzzled at her neck and hair. Sita's eyelids fluttered. Lexi, Juniper, Violet, and Sorrel raced over.

"No!" screamed Lizzie.

Mia tugged frantically at the creepers covering Sita's mouth. If Sita could speak, she could use her magic.

Lizzie grabbed a handful of pine needles from the ground and tossed them into the air.

"Help Sita!" Mia gasped to the others as pine needles started to swirl up in a tornado again. "I'll make a magic shield."

She pictured a shield around them, protecting them. Triumph rushed through her as she saw a silvery bubble form around her friends and their animals. The pine needles battered against it, scratching and scraping, but the shield stayed strong, and the needles dropped harmlessly to the ground.

Sita started to sit up. "What's happening?"

she said in confusion, peering through the silvery shield. "Why is Lizzie here?"

"We'll explain later," said Violet quickly. "All you need to know is that she's bad!"

Lizzie scrambled to her feet. "That shield won't protect you from me!" she snarled. "A shield cast by a single 10 year old, inexperienced in using magic?" She shook her head and uncorked the silver bottle. She walked toward them. "Pathetic! One drop of this and it will dissolve instantly."

Mia's mind was working frantically. "But it's not cast just by a single 10 year old!" She turned to the others. "Everyone, help me like we helped Sita before!" Mia didn't need to say any more—the others instantly understood. They all reached out and touched her.

Mia felt them draw on the magic current around them, and they started channeling it into her. It flowed strongly. She felt wonderfully powerful as she focused on the shield. Suddenly, it started to glow. Rainbow colors streamed across its surface, and light sparked off it just as Lizzie threw the contents of the bottle.

The potion hit the surface and rebounded, splashing all over Lizzie. She screamed and collapsed on the ground, changing back into Elizabeth as she did so. Sita gasped in shock. "She's Elizabeth!" The others nodded as the plants instantly released their grip on the girls.

"What have you done?" Elizabeth panted hoarsely, glaring at them from the ground. "I can't move!"

"What's happening?" Mia said to Bracken.

"I don't know," he said.

"I believe I do! It's the threefold rule of magic," said Sorrel. "The evil she intended when she threw the potion has returned to her three times as strongly. The binding spell has tripled in power." She looked smugly at Elizabeth. "Now she can't do anything without your command."

"No!" screamed Elizabeth.

The girls looked at each other. Mia broke the connection with the current, and the bubble evaporated into a shower of glittery sparkles. "What do we do?" she said to the others.

"I don't want her under our command," said Lexi.

"Leave this to me," said Violet. She walked over to Elizabeth. "We command you to leave Westport," she said firmly. "You must never be Lizzie again. You must stay as Elizabeth, and you must only use your magic for good from now on. If you do anything else, you will … you will … explode!" she finished.

"Explode?" Mia exclaimed, glancing at Elizabeth, who looked horrified.

Violet grinned. "I couldn't think of anything else."

"I'm really glad Sita is the one who usually does the commanding," said Lexi. Sita gave her a weak smile. "But yes, I guess you're right in this case. You must be good from now on and get older like regular people do," she told Elizabeth.

"Now get up and go home without saying anything," said Violet. "Oh, and I also command you to give your cat some treats. It's not his fault that you used magic on him."

Glaring at her, Elizabeth got to her feet. With a toss of her hair, she turned and stalked off into the trees, the cat following at her heels.

"We did it!" said Violet, looking at the others as the animals jumped around them—barking, meowing, bleating, and chattering.

"Will someone please tell me what's going on?" asked Sita in confusion.

They quickly explained.

"So Elizabeth was Lizzie and Lizzie was Elizabeth all along?" Sita shook her head in astonishment. "Elizabeth was doing the dark magic?" She rubbed her head. "Ouch. I have a huge bump on my head. I wish I could heal myself, but healing magic only works on other people."

Willow inspected the bump. "It should get better soon."

"And I guess it's definitely worth having a bump if it means we've stopped the dark magic," said Sita, petting her.

"I told you we were right to come into the clearing and see what was going on," Violet said to Lexi.

"Right?" spluttered Lexi. "We were almost bound to do her bidding forever!"

"It was very scary!" said Juniper, taking a flying leap onto Lexi's head.

"It wasn't that bad," said Violet airily. She nudged Mia. "Thanks for coming after me."

"No prob, but next time, maybe let's think about it at least for a few seconds first," said Mia.

"Maybe," said Violet with a grin. "Maybe not."

"Look, everyone!" said Sita. "Look what's happening!"

All around them, the clearing was healing itself. The withered trees straightened up, green leaves sprouting on their branches and pine needles reappearing on the branches. Bright daffodils pushed up through the ground, and the waterfall started to flow with sparkling water that rushed over the stones and down to the ocean in a glittering stream. Birds swooped through the branches.

"It looks beautiful!" said Willow.

"It's the threefold rule again," said Sorrel, walking around the clearing. "The good you've just done has come back threefold. The magic has been strengthened so much that the clearing is rejuvenating and returning to normal."

Bracken barked in excitement. Willow bucked, and Juniper raced up the tree trunks and leaped from branch to branch.

"We did it! We did it!" said Mia, grabbing

Violet's hands and swinging her around. She imagined her grandma smiling down at her from wherever she was and knew she would be feeling very proud. "We saved the clearing!"

"And we did some awesome magic together!" said Violet happily.

"There's always something new to learn about magic," said Lexi. "That's why I love it so much."

"Me, too." Mia smiled. "I can't wait to learn even more!" She held out her arms, and Bracken jumped into them.

"Whatever comes along next, we'll be ready for it," he said, licking her nose.

"Ready and waiting," Mia agreed, hugging him tightly.

A week later, the girls stood on the street by the path watching the last of Elizabeth's possessions being loaded into a moving truck. None of them had seen Elizabeth since the evening in the woods. According to Mia's mom, she'd decided she couldn't live so far away from New York, so the family had moved back.

The totally made-up, pretend family, Mia thought.

"I wonder what will happen to your grandma's house now," Sita said to Mia. "Hopefully someone nice will move in."

"Elizabeth seemed nice," said Mia. She shook her head. "It's so hard to tell with people, isn't it? You meet someone and think one thing about them, and then they turn out to be totally different."

"Like Mrs. Sands," said Violet. "She's been much friendlier this week."

"I went into the office when she was there and used my magic to heal her back," said Sita. "My nana says Mrs. Sands thinks she's feeling better because she got some new medicine from the doctor. I don't mind what she thinks. I'm just glad she's happier now. It was the pain that was making her so grumpy."

"I feel bad that we suspected her," said Lexi. "It's difficult to know who to trust, though."

Mia linked arms with her. "We can trust each other. At least we know that."

"And Sorrel, Bracken, Willow, and Juniper," added Violet.

"Let's go to the clearing and see them," said Sita eagerly. "We can try combining our magic again."

"And I want to try making a magic barrier again," said Lexi. "I'm sure I'll be able to do it one day if I keep practicing."

"Race you all there!" Mia said.

She set off down the path, pushing through the undergrowth and bursting out into the clearing. It looked very different from how it did a few weeks ago. The waterfall was rushing merrily over the rocks, the water glinting in the sunlight. The trees' branches were covered with new leaves, bluebells carpeted the forest floor among the tree trunks, and swaths of pretty pink flowers edged the soft grass of the clearing. The air smelled fresh and sweet.

The girls called their animals' names. Bracken, Willow, Juniper, and Sorrel appeared, jumping and skipping around the girls.

Happiness rushed through Mia as Bracken bounded into her arms, his beautiful indigo eyes shining. "Is it magic time, Mia?" he asked eagerly.

Mia grinned and kissed him on the nose. "Oh, yes!" she said. "It always is!"